Niko & Kate

Fawn Michelle Goodman

illustrated by **Rich Green**

PUPPET SHOW PRESS

NEW YORK, NEW YORK

www.puppetshowpress.com

Above tree-covered hills,
in a peaceful gnome village,

there lived a loving and
generous gnome family.

They had a gnome daughter
named Kate who loved to read
old gnome books and learn new
gnome things.

Niko was very smart,
just like his
gnome sister, Kate.
They both did
well in school.

Unfortunately, some of the gnome kids at the gnome school were afraid of Niko because he was different...

... but not Kate, she loved her brother very much.

Niko and Kate did everything together.

One day, Niko decided to tell Kate a secret.

He knew his sister would understand.

As summer arrived in the gnome village, the town was mysteriously overwhelmed by exotic vines. They covered all of the gnome homes, the gnome trees, the gnome bridges, and even the gnome roads.

The villagers sprung into action...

They tried cutting the vines
with their gnome axes.

They tried burning the vines
with their gnome torches.

They tried poisoning the vines with their gnome potions.

They even tried pulling out the vines with their gnome hands.

Nothing worked.

The vines kept coming back and growing bigger and **bigger** and **bigger**.

Soon they blocked out the sun.

The gnomes began to panic. They needed a solution fast.

Suddenly, Kate had an idea.

"Niko, if you're willing to reveal your
secret, you can help us get rid of the vines!"

Niko's secret was a great source
of embarrassment for him.
He wasn't like other vampires.

Instead of turning into a bat,
he transformed into...

...AN ELEPHANT!

"Be brave, Niko, we need your help!
Use your trunk to pull up the roots and eat up all the
vines so they won't grow back."

Niko shoved the vines into his mouth.

Loud crunching and chewing noises
were heard throughout the village.

When he was finished,
Niko lay exhausted and full.

"Niko and Kate, you did it!"
Everyone in the village was very grateful.

Niko and Kate were
happy to have helped.

The gnome children
were suddenly curious
about Niko's trunk and how
Niko was able to save them.

From that day on,
the village knew they could count on Niko and Kate.

To my little gnomes, and one medium-large elf.
F.M.G.

To R, C, C, M, D, M and A
R.G.

First edition 2016

Cover and layout design: Rich Green

Library of Congress Control Number: 2016943485
ISBN: 978-0-998-00830-1

Printed in PRC

PUPPET
SHOW
PRESS

NEW YORK, NEW YORK
www.puppetshowpress.com